This book belongs to:

....

ISBN 978-1-84135-197-1

Published by Award Publications Limited,
The Old Riding School, The Welbeck Estate,
Worksop, Nottinghamshire, S80 3LR

www.awardpublications.co.uk

10 3

Printed in Malaysia

Award Young Readers

The Three Little Kittens

Rewritten by Jackie Andrews
Illustrated by Lesley Smith

AWARD PUBLICATIONS LIMITED

Once there were three little kittens called Daisy, Maisy and Bo. They lived with their mother in a tiny house on top of a hill.

One day, a parcel arrived from their grand-mother. Inside were three new coats; a blue coat for Daisy, a red coat for Maisy and a yellow coat for Bo. The three kittens put them on.

"Miaow! Aren't we smart?" they cried.

"Yes, indeed," purred their mother. "I'll have to knit you all some mittens, now, to wear with your new coats."

She finished them that very week: blue mittens for Daisy, red mittens for Maisy and yellow mittens for Bo. The three little kittens were very happy and proud of their new outfits.

"Take care of your mittens, won't you?" said their mother. "Mind you don't lose them!"

Day after day, the three little kittens wore their mittens every time they left the house. But one day, *catastrophe*! They ran to their mother with tears in their eyes.

"Mama, Mama!" they cried. "We've lost our mittens. Whatever shall we do?"

Their mother was busy making a delicious blackberry pie. She turned to look at her three kittens and frowned. "You've lost your mittens? You naughty kittens!" she scolded. "Then you shall have no pie."

"Miaow!"

Daisy, Maisy and Bo wiped their eyes and blew their noses on their handkerchiefs. Then they went to look for their mittens.

First, they went to the chicken coop, where a fat brown hen was sitting on her eggs.

"Have you seen our mittens, Clucky Hen?" they asked.

"Cluck, cluck, cluck," said Clucky Hen. "No, I haven't seen your mittens. Have you looked in your pockets?"

Daisy, Maisy and Bo pulled everything out of their pockets and shook their heads.

"Miaow! No mittens there," they said.

Next, the three little kittens searched their bedroom. They looked in all the cupboards and drawers, and under all the beds.

"Miaow! No mittens there!"

Then they climbed up into the attic to look
in a chest full of old clothes.

"This is a silly place to look," said Bo. "We
haven't been up here for ages."

But it was good fun, exploring.

They tried hard to remember all the places they had been in the last two days.

"We've only been to the wood to pick blackberries," said Maisy.

"And that's where they are!" cried Daisy. "They're hanging on the bushes!"

"That's right," said Bo. "We took them off to pick the blackberries."

The three little kittens scooted away to the wood. And there were the red, blue and yellow mittens, hanging from the blackberry bushes just where they had left them.

The kittens snatched them up and ran home to tell their mother.

"Put on your mittens, you silly kittens," she said with a laugh, "and you shall have some pie."

"This is the tastiest blackberry pie I've ever eaten," said Maisy.

"It's the juiciest blackberry pie I've ever eaten," said Daisy.

"Oh no!" said Bo. "Just look at our mittens!"

The three little kittens ran to show their
mother their messy, sticky mittens.

"You silly kittens," she said. "You should have taken off your mittens to eat your pie."

"Miaow! What shall we do?" they cried.

"You must wash your mittens," said their mother, "and hang them out to dry. Then they'll be as good as new."

Maisy fetched the washtub. Daisy found the washing-powder. Bo brought the pegbag and washing-basket. They filled the washtub with warm water. Then they tipped in some washing powder and swished it round to make bubbles.

In went their mittens.

Wash, wash, wash, went the three little kittens until all the blackberry stains had disappeared and their mittens were bright blue, red and yellow again.

They hung them on the clothes-line to dry.

"Look, Mama!" The three little kittens held up their soft, fluffy mittens. Daisy wore blue, Maisy wore red and Bo wore yellow.

Their mother smiled at them.

"Such clean mittens," she said, "and such clever kittens. You've had a very busy day. It's time for three little kittens to be fast asleep now."

Daisy, Maisy and Bo climbed into their basket and snuggled up together. Soon they were fast asleep and dreaming of blackberry pie. *Purr, purr, purr.*

The Three Little Kittens

Three little kittens, they lost their mittens,
And they began to cry,
Oh, Mother dear, we sadly fear
That we have lost our mittens.
What! Lost your mittens, you naughty kittens!
Then you shall have no pie!
Miaow, miaow, miaow,
No, you shall have no pie!

The three little kittens, they found their mittens,
And they began to cry,
Oh, Mother dear, see here, see here,
For we have found our mittens.
Put on your mittens, you silly kittens,
And you shall have some pie.
Purr, purr, purr,
Oh, let us have some pie.